SOCCER SUPERSTARS

SOCCER SUPERSTARS

David Bedford

Illustrated by
Keith Brumpton

LITTLE HARE
www.littleharebooks.com

Little Hare Books
an imprint of
Hardie Grant Egmont
85 High Street
Prahran, Victoria 3181, Australia

www.littleharebooks.com

First published 2010

National Library of Australia
Cataloguing-in-Publication entry

Bedford, David, 1969-

Soccer Superstars / David Bedford; illustrator, Keith Brumpton.

978 1 921541 28 5 (pbk.)

Bedford, David, 1969- Team; 8.

For primary school age.

Soccer stories.

Brumpton, Keith.

823.92

Cover design by Xou Creative (www.xou.com.au)
Set in 13.5/21 pt Giovanni by Clinton Ellicott
Printed through Polskabooks
Printed at Rzeszow Zaklady Graficzne, Rzeszow, Poland,
March 2010

5 4 3 2 1

For Victor Daniels,
Captain of the Odds and Ends Allied
football team, Colombo 1942–1944
DB

Prof
Gertie

Darren   Harvey

Rita   Matt   Steffi   Mark 1

Chapter 1

It was Saturday morning, and the sun was shining. Harvey left home with his favourite football tucked under his arm.

When he reached the pitch, he found his team mates lounging in the centre circle. Darren lay on his back, his goalkeeper's gloves behind his head. He was smiling and chewing a blade of grass.

"I'm a Superstar," he explained, opening one eye to peer at Harvey, who laughed.

"Me too," chuckled Rita.

"Bliss," said Steffi, angling her face to the sun.

"Rockin' and rollin'," said Matt, who was eating a banana. He hurled the empty skin away across the pitch, causing a seagull to take flight. "I'll pick it up later," he said lazily, as Rita frowned at him.

Harvey bounced his ball. "Shall we get started?"

Rita stood up, but nobody else moved.

"Come on," urged Harvey, "we might not have a game today, but even Superstars need to practise."

"Okay," yawned Darren. "I'm not doing warm-ups, though. They're boring."

Harvey was about to protest, then decided there was no need. The Team were on a winning streak, and what's more, they had just beaten a major record.

Darren had found out all about it.

"It's called the *Superstars* record," he had told them the previous week, after they'd just thrashed the Diamonds four-nil. "The team with the longest run of unbeaten matches are called *Superstars*."

He held up a picture from an old newspaper he'd got from the library. It showed the team who had previously held the record — the Odds and Ends. The headline was just one word: "Superstars".

The Team had been delighted that they were the new Superstars. Harvey was sure their unbeaten run would go on for ages, especially when he found out who they were playing in their next match.

It was the Odds and Ends! Even though they'd won the record themselves years ago, they were now stuck at the bottom of the league. The Team would beat them easily — whether they warmed up or not.

"Let's play Defenders," Harvey told The Team. His friends split into two groups, one to defend Darren's goal, the other to attack it.

Darren kicked the ball out with a triumphant shout of, "WE ARE *SUPERSTARS!*"

And at that moment, everything began to go wrong.

Steffi and Matt both jumped for the ball, but missed it and headed each other. *THUNK!*

Rita, trotting backwards into space, twisted her ankle. "AAARGH!"

And then Harvey took a shot at goal, and watched the ball snap the crossbar into two pieces. *CRACK!*

Harvey looked around at The Team's stunned faces.

"Your ball's burst, too!" exclaimed Darren, bringing Harvey's ball over, so they could see the splinter of wood sticking from it. "And look," he added, bowing his head so Harvey could see a white line running through his hair.

"Stylish," said Steffi, sounding impressed.

"Kind of stylish," said Rita, sounding unsure.

"It's *seagull poo*," said Darren. "And I only washed my hair the other day."

Darren looked around The Team anxiously. "I've got something to tell you," he said. "It's about the Superstars record. I think it might be jinxed."

"What does that mean?" said Harvey, impatiently tugging the splinter from his ball.

"A jinx is bad news," said Matt solemnly. "The Rockton Rovers had a travel jinx last season. They lost every game they played away from home."

"The Superstars jinx is worse," said Darren.

"Ever since the Odds and Ends won the record, they've lost every game they've played."

"That's not because of a jinx," Harvey said. "Everyone knows the Odds and Ends are useless because they're not a proper team. Whoever turns up on the day gets to play for them. That's why they're called the Odds and Ends."

Harvey had played for the Odds and Ends himself before he formed The Team, and he hadn't enjoyed it. His team mates had all been strangers who didn't know how to play together.

"The Odds and Ends *were* good once, though," countered Rita. "They had to be, because they won the record."

Harvey scratched his chin. There had to be some other explanation for the Odds and Ends becoming so bad. Harvey didn't believe in jinxes.

"They must have been jinxed," insisted Matt.

"And now we hold the record," said Rita, biting her lip. "The jinx is on us."

The Team looked devastated.

"I'm sure we'll be all right," said Harvey, trying to sound cheerful. "Nothing can stop The Team — we're Superstars, remember?"

Steffi rounded on him. "What's the point in being called Superstars if we're going to lose every week?" she said angrily.

"I don't want to be rubbish," said Darren.

"Nobody does," said Rita.

"That's it, then," said Matt. He picked up his kitbag and slung it over his shoulder.

"What do you mean?" said Harvey.

"The Team is finished," said Matt. "We've been jinxed. There's nothing we can do about it, apart from stop playing altogether."

Chapter 2

"We can't give up!" Harvey said. He couldn't believe what he'd just heard. "We've worked too hard on The Team to walk away now!"

The Team looked uncomfortable, and Harvey knew why. They'd put in a lot of effort this season, and their longer training sessions had paid off. That's why they'd won the Superstars record — because they deserved to.

"We've just had a few training hiccups," Harvey said soothingly. "It's not a jinx — accidents happen all the time."

"Not when I'm wearing my lucky Ballerinas," snapped Steffi. She held up her bright-pink designer football boots.

"And not when I'm wearing my lucky gloves," said Darren. "They're less comfortable than my new ones, but they are seriously lucky."

"I ate my lucky banana before we started," commented Matt. "I never set foot on a pitch without it. The record must be so unlucky, our lucky charms have no power against it."

"Why have you all got lucky charms?" said Harvey surprised. "The Team doesn't need them."

Rita pulled a scrap of yellow cloth from inside one of her socks. "This is from my baby blanket," she said, blushing. "It's my luckiest thing. Everyone needs a lucky charm."

"I don't," said Harvey.

"Haven't you got a lucky object, Harv?" said Darren, amazed.

Harvey shook his head. The Team looked shocked.

"You need to keep luck on your side, mate," Darren advised.

"Absolute tosh!" said a voice from the side of the pitch.

Harvey turned to see Professor Gertie, The Team's number-one fan, walking towards them. Her greatest invention, the football-playing robot, Mark 1, trotted along beside her. Mark 1 was a football genius, and had been The Team's trainer ever since he was banned from playing in matches because robots were against the rules.

"Re-fresshh-mentz!" chimed Mark 1.

Harvey saw that the robot was holding a tray with a stack of cups, straws, and a full jug of lemonade on it.

Harvey felt relieved to see Professor Gertie. She always did her best to help The Team.

"It's not tosh, Professor," said Rita, "we need good luck to play, especially now we've been jinxed, and — look out!"

Harvey saw the danger at the same time as Rita, but it was too late. Mark 1's foot came down on Matt's banana skin, and he slipped. Both of his feet flipped upwards, and the tray, cups, straws and jug spun into the air.

Professor Gertie covered her head with her arms as lemonade rained down.

"More bad luck," groaned Darren.

And then, to Harvey's astonishment, he saw Mark 1's fall turn into a back flip. The robot's feet spun around to the ground and, with a metallic jingle, he stood up. One hand shot out to catch the tray, the half-full jug of lemonade, the cups, and then the straws.

"Re-fresshh-mentz," chimed Mark 1, again, as if nothing had happened. "Come an' get 'em!"

Darren whooped. "How *lucky* was that!"

"He hardly spilled a drop," breathed Stelh.

The Team crowded around the robot. Mark 1 began pouring drinks and handing them out. But Steffi was more interested in the little objects that the Football Machine was wearing on chains around his neck. They were pale grey shapes with silver lines swirling through them.

"Are those . . . lucky charms?" She turned to Darren. "They'll make us lucky, like Mark 1!"

Professor Gertie snorted. "Those things are merely barebones," she said, as if that explained everything.

Harvey was about to ask what barebones were, when Mark 1 began giving them out. Steffi swapped hers with Matt's. Darren held one up to examine it, beaming as if he'd just found treasure. Rita glanced guiltily at Harvey and then hung one around her neck.

Professor Gertie had her hands on her hips. "As a scientist," she declared, "I can assure you there is no such thing as luck. Everything that happens has a simple explanation in fact."

Harvey was about to agree with her when he noticed something odd.

The Team were smiling as if all of their worries had been taken away.

"They're already more confident," he said, thinking aloud.

Professor Gertie stared at him. "Harvey," she said sternly, "are you telling me *you* believe in jinxes and lucky charms?"

"Er, no," said Harvey truthfully. "I don't. It's just that Mark 1's barebones seem to make The Team feel better."

Harvey had an idea. He threw his burst ball towards Steffi, who saw it coming late and backheeled it. Matt flicked it into the air, and Darren punched it on to Rita.

Harvey watched with satisfaction as Mark 1 joined in the kickabout.

Harvey felt a surge of relief. The Team were playing again. Mark 1 had saved the day!

Then he noticed that Professor Gertie was watching The Team in a strange way. It was as if she was seeing them for the last time.

"Professor?" Harvey said, in concern. "What's wrong? The Team are only wearing some bits of metal, aren't they? It doesn't matter."

"It does matter," Professor Gertie replied huffily. "The Team have decided to turn their back on science. They have put their faith in mumbo-jumbo nonsense instead. I have no option but to withdraw my services."

Hugging her lab coat to her, she left without looking back.

Chapter 3

Harvey woke up early on Sunday morning with only one thing on his mind: he had to get Professor Gertie back. She was just as much a part of The Team as any player. And she had never let them down.

Suddenly, Harvey ducked under his pillow as a blaring sound rattled his window.

Then he heard Darren shout, "Cut it out! He'll be awake by now!"

The noise stopped.

Harvey opened his curtains and saw that

The Team were standing on the street below. They were huddled beside Mark 1. The robot was holding an odd-looking trumpet to his metal lips. He waved happily at Harvey.

Professor Gertie, who was Harvey's neighbour, leaned out from a window halfway up her inventing tower. "What is it?" she said sleepily. "Did something of mine explode?"

"No, Professor," called Darren. "Your metal man has been around to all of our houses and woken everyone up!"

Professor Gertie spotted the robot and surveyed The Team. Then to Harvey's dismay, she closed her window with a bang. Clearly, she was still cross about the barebones, and wanted nothing more to do with The Team.

Mark 1 tucked the trumpet under his arm and said pleasantly, "Key-eep onn!"

The Team grumbled.

"If he says that one more time . . ." threatened Steffi.

"It's how he got us out of bed," Rita called

up to Harvey. "You'd better get dressed and come out. If you don't, he'll blow the bugle again. He woke up my whole street!"

Harvey hurried outside. His breath made clouds in the chilly air.

"Key-eep onn!" said the robot again, and bounded away down the path.

Harvey and The Team followed.

"It's been like this for the last hour," said Rita as they jogged along steadily. "He's had us running all over the place!"

The robot led them up a hill, away from Harvey's house.

"This isn't the way to the pitch," Harvey commented.

"What *is* this way?" demanded Steffi.

"A nature trail," said Harvey. "It goes out into the countryside."

"Oh, great!" Steffi growled, looking down at her clean flip-flops.

"Maybe it's a new kind of training session," Harvey suggested hopefully.

"Well, I'm only here because Mark 1 gave us those lucky charms," said Steffi. She showed Harvey her heart-shaped barebone. It had a tiny "M1" stamped on it.

Harvey looked around, and saw that every member of The Team was wearing a barebone.

"We think Mark 1 has got other lucky things to show us," said Rita.

"Yeah," said Darren, "I reckon he's got a knack for being lucky. I mean, the way he recovered his balance after slipping on Matt's banana skin was . . ." Darren waved his arms in circles. He seemed unable to find the right word. "And his lucky charms protect us from the Superstars jinx," he added.

"I haven't had *any* bad luck since I got my barebone," agreed Steffi.

"If you want a theory," butted in Matt, "I'd say my banana skin *made* that robot lucky. What he was wearing became lucky, too. Before he slipped, he was just wearing junk. Afterwards, the junk got *luck energy*."

"He's a lucky robot!" said Rita, chuckling.

Harvey sighed. So that was why The Team were following the robot. They were all hoping for more good luck.

Harvey's feet squelched in mushy leaves as they reached the nature trail. He knew that if the path was wet here, it would be impossibly muddy further ahead.

He was about to warn Mark 1 that the way would be blocked, when the robot sped up with a mechanical, "Key-eep onn!"

Harvey had the feeling it was going to be a long morning.

Harvey felt his feet sinking into the thick, slimy mud and began to lose his balance. Darren tried to hold him up, but skidded sideways. Both of them sat down heavily with a *splat*!

Rita grabbed Darren's arms and tried pulling him out. "This mud's like quicksand!" she said, straining. "The more I pull, the deeper I sink!" She fell forwards onto her knees.

Harvey looked around for help and saw Mark 1 standing at the far side of the mud. He was watching calmly as The Team struggled.

Matt was lying on his belly and pushing himself across the mud with his elbows. It looked to Harvey as if he was learning to swim.

Steffi had a different idea. She waited back on the path, holding her flip-flops in the air. "Would somebody please help me across?" she asked. "Mud's not really my thing."

Harvey had an idea. "Step on Matt," he told Steffi. "And then on Darren." He pointed out a route across the mud.

"I'm not a stepping stone!" yelped Matt.

Steffi ignored him and crawled lightly across his back. She knelt on Darren's legs and helped Harvey claw Rita from the mud. Then, Steffi, Harvey and Rita lay across Darren to rescue Matt, who was now doing backstroke but getting nowhere.

After a long struggle, The Team gathered together on the far side of the mud. They were gasping for breath.

"That was —" began Darren.

Before he could finish, Mark 1 sprang away. "Key-eep onn!" he said.

The Team hurried after the robot.

Harvey spotted a stream ahead. "It's too deep to cross," he said.

The robot sped up. Harvey heard Mark 1's motors whirring as he accelerated to the nearest bank.

Then, with a *boing!*, Mark 1 bounced high through the air. Harvey saw the sun glinting on the springs of Mark 1's built-in Bouncing Boots, before the robot landed on the far side.

There was no way any of The Team could follow that. "Wait for us!" called Harvey, but the Football Machine kept running.

Rita surveyed the stream. "It's too wide for us to jump," she said.

"But if we were lucky . . ." Darren took six steps back. Then he ran and jumped. He landed on the far bank, teetered on the edge, then fell forwards onto dry land.

The Team cheered. Rita went next. She landed on one foot on the far side, and Darren caught her. Soon the rest of The Team had made it across — all except Harvey.

"Come on, mate!" said Darren. "You'll be fine, just like we were!"

Harvey took twelve steps back. Then he put his head down, sprinted as fast as he could — and tripped on a loose stone.

"Aaargh!" called Harvey as he tumbled into the cold stream. He felt his friends' hands dragging him out.

Harvey did his best to shake himself dry. Then he heard Mark 1 call, "Key-eep onn!" from far off, and he had to squelch after The Team.

They finally stopped at the top of a steep hill. Rita shielded her eyes with her hand and looked around. "Where's Mark 1 gone? I can't see him," she said.

Harvey surveyed the hills and woods. There was no sign of the robot.

"Which way is home?" said Darren.

The Team pointed in different directions.

"Oh, wonderful!" said Steffi sarcastically.

By the time the team mates found their way back to Harvey's house, the sun was setting behind Professor Gertie's inventing tower.

"Why did Mark 1 lead us out into the countryside and abandon us like that?" said Rita. She sounded how Harvey felt — exhausted.

"Maybe it was a test," Harvey suggested. "To see if we had enough stamina to get back."

"It's got nothing to do with stamina, mate," said Darren, tapping his barebone. "These lucky charms helped us find our way home. Mark 1 is showing us how powerful they are, so we don't worry about the Superstars jinx."

"They're awesome," agreed Steffi.

"Unbeatable," said Matt.

"They really do work," Rita told Harvey. "I'm sure of it."

The Team drifted down the hill towards their homes, kissing their barebones.

"*Tsk! Tsk!*" said Professor Gertie. She was standing in the tower's shadow.

"There you are!" said Harvey. "I've wanted to ask you all day — will you please come back to support The Team? I promise I don't believe in barebones — or jinxes."

"I'm afraid my mind is made up," Professor Gertie said softly. "I can only use my scientific creativity for teams who believe in it."

A terrible thought popped into Harvey's head. "You don't mean you're helping *another team*, do you?"

"Yes," said Professor Gertie. "From now on, I will be working on a new team."

And she went inside, leaving Harvey gaping after her.

Chapter 4

At school the following week, Harvey did everything he could to convince Darren to give up his barebone. Darren spent most of the time with his hands over his ears, not listening.

On Thursday, Harvey decided to make his argument clear by writing a note in Darren's workbook. He wrote:

There are no such things as jinxes! Things just happen!

If The Team don't put away the barebones, we'll lose Professor Gertie!

Darren read the note, then pointed at Harvey's shoes, which were almost falling off his feet because both of his laces had snapped. Then he pointed at Harvey's nose, which was yellow because Harvey had bumped into a freshly painted door.

"*You* need to get lucky, mate," said Darren.

Harvey had to admit he'd had an unfortunate

week, but that didn't mean he had to start believing in jinxes or other things that weren't real. He decided to try to persuade The Team to give up their barebones that night at training. By the afternoon, however, snow had begun to fall.

Darren pointed at Harvey, and then out of the window.

"*I* didn't make it snow!" Harvey told him.

"It's the middle of spring," said Darren. "It must be somebody's fault."

"We can train tomorrow," insisted Harvey.

As he spoke, he could tell that Darren was thinking that the next day would bring floods, or earthquakes, or a tornado on their pitch.

To Harvey's relief, Friday was warm and sunny. The snow melted as fast as it had arrived, and all seemed well.

Even Darren had little to complain about. Harvey did trip over while carrying his lunch tray, but he was able to scrape most of his food back onto his plate. And he kept out of trouble for the rest of the day, apart from accidentally getting locked in a cupboard.

The serious problems began when he met The Team after school for training. Mark 1 was

there — and so was Masher, the monstrous crab-like machine Professor Gertie had designed to grind up useless inventions.

"What's *that* doing here?" Darren said, keeping his distance from the monster.

Harvey did the same. Professor Gertie claimed that Masher was harmless, and she had even given him to Mark 1 for a pet. But Masher's claw looked dangerously sharp.

Luckily, Harvey thought, Mark 1 was gripping Masher's lead tightly.

Rita bounced a brand-new ball. "We can use this from now on," she said. "My dad got it for us." She tossed the ball to Matt.

Masher strained at his lead, his huge claw snapping . . .

And then Mark 1 let him go.

The Team scattered. Masher tore towards Matt, who hurriedly kicked the ball away.

Masher lurched after it.

"He wants my ball!" yelled Rita in outrage. "Mark 1 — call him off!"

Mark 1 didn't blink, and Rita pelted after the ball. She reached it before Masher did and toe-poked it to Harvey, who spun into action. He hoofed the ball long to Darren. The Team's goalie caught it, waited for Masher to get near, and then hurled it to Steffi.

Matt began to cheer every pass.

Masher chased the ball without stopping until the sun set and the streetlights came on. Finally, Mark 1 gave a short whistle. Masher trotted obediently back to his owner, and the two left without a word.

Harvey bent over, panting. "At least Masher didn't get the ball," he said, trying to smile at Rita. "We had to work hard, though!"

Rita looked troubled. "We were lucky. At least, most of us were."

She was looking at Harvey's sleeve. Masher had nipped at it and torn a ragged hole. It was the only damage done to The Team — and of course, Harvey thought, it had to happen to him.

"We've got a problem, mate," Darren said, as The Team gathered around.

Harvey had the feeling they'd already planned to talk to him, even before he had arrived for training. "Don't say you won't play in Saturday's match," he said, guessing that they were still nervous about the jinx. "You haven't been unlucky all training session."

"*We* aren't unlucky," agreed Steffi, "but *you* are!"

"We've thought about it," said Darren. "And if you want The Team to keep going, then . . ."

Darren didn't want to finish, but Matt said it for him.

"You can't play, Harv," he said. "You don't have a barebone, or anything."

"If we win the next match with our lucky charms," Darren explained, "we'll beat the jinx for good. The Team will *stay* lucky."

"Then you can come back," said Rita. "You'll only have to sit out one game."

Harvey couldn't take it in. "I'm on The Team," he said. "Aren't I?"

"Not tomorrow," said Steffi.

To Harvey's horror, all of his team mates nodded in agreement.

Harvey wandered home in a daze, hardly able to believe what his friends had told him.

He found himself standing outside Professor Gertie's tower. The door was open. Through it, Harvey saw Mark 1 sitting in a chair.

He was wearing a brightly coloured robe and he had his feet up on the kitchen table.

Professor Gertie was bending over the robot's toes as if she was painting his nails, but instead of a brush, she held a screwdriver.

Harvey was making a move to step inside when a gurgle from under the table told him that he'd been spotted by Masher. The monster's eyes rotated towards him menacingly. Harvey backed off along the garden path, without Mark 1 or Professor Gertie having seen him.

Harvey stood by himself in the dark. He'd never felt so alone. His team had abandoned him, and Professor Gertie and Mark 1 were unreachable.

The moon drifted out from behind a cloud and illuminated Mark 1's kit hanging on a clothes line. The robot's red shirt, white shorts and red socks had been pegged out. So had a pair of white undershorts with pink footballs dotted all over them. If Harvey hadn't felt so miserable, he might have laughed. He'd had no idea the robot wore those.

Something else on the clothes line caught Harvey's attention. It was one last barebone,

glistening like a jewel as it twirled in the breeze. Harvey suddenly remembered what Darren had said.

You need to get lucky.

He took a step forward. Then he stopped. It still didn't make sense. How could wearing something special make you lucky? Harvey was sure it couldn't. It was a shame The Team didn't understand that.

Harvey didn't move. He didn't know what to do.

At last, he made up his mind. He reached silently towards the clothes line.

Chapter 5

On Saturday afternoon, when Harvey strode on to the Odds and Ends' pitch, Steffi barred his way.

"Harvey," she said. "You're not on The Team today. We've told you why — if you play, we can't beat the jinx."

Harvey lowered his shorts.

The Team goggled at him.

"You're wearing great big funny pants," said Darren curiously.

"They're Mark 1's undershorts," explained Harvey. The Team peered more closely.

"Wow," said Matt in awe. "*Anything* Mark 1 wears will beat the jinx!"

"It's good to have you back, mate." Darren held out his hand, and Harvey shook it.

The rest of The Team nodded, and Harvey felt a rush of excitement. This match was one of the most important The Team had ever played. They had to win it to put their worries about the Superstars jinx behind them. The survival of The Team depended on it.

He turned to where the Odds and Ends were arriving. They looked a raggle-taggle bunch and were dressed in all kinds of mismatched kit. Then he saw Professor Gertie standing in her usual spot on the sidelines. Mark 1 stood next to her.

"I knew she'd get over us wearing barebones," said Darren, nudging Harvey.

Harvey wasn't sure. Professor Gertie was not wearing her usual Team supporters' scarf and hat. Instead, she wore an old lab coat. The Football Machine wore his robe.

While The Team warmed up, Harvey trotted over to Professor Gertie, keen to find out what was going on. "Are you supporting the Odds and Ends?" he asked her meekly. "I would understand — The Team have let you down."

Professor Gertie tutted. "If you think I am going to support anyone but The Team, Harvey, you'd better reboot!" she said.

"But you said you were using your science for another team," Harvey insisted.

"Ah," said Professor Gertie. She grinned and put her arm around the robot. "You mean Mark 1."

"Pardon?" said Harvey, confused. "Mark 1 isn't a *team*, is he, Professor?"

"In a manner of speaking," she replied, "he is. My robot now has the full benefit of my scientific capabilities. I am proud to reveal that Mark 1 — who has been a Work in Progress for a long time — is now fully finished." She raised her voice and declared, "Say hello to my *All-in-One Team Machine*!"

Mark 1 threw off his robe dramatically.

Harvey looked the robot up and down, unsure what he was supposed to see. Mark 1 was dressed in The Team's old white top and red shorts. The shirt seemed too small for him, but apart from that, he looked just the same.

"He is equipped with new, state-of-the-art super-enhancements," Professor Gertie said as the robot began warming up. The Team crowded around to watch.

"Firstly," said Professor Gertie, "you are already aware of Mark 1's Belly Balance Button. It stops him falling over, no matter what.

Even," she added, with a scowl towards Matt, "when he slips on a banana skin!"

Matt looked at the ground, his face reddening.

"Secondly," said Professor Gertie, "Mark 1 now has a fully integrated Over Throw. It allows his throw-ins to reach any location on the pitch."

That's why his shirt looks tight, thought Harvey. The Football Machine's got muscles.

"The Over Throw mechanism includes Rapid Reflexes," Professor Gertie continued, "which are for goalkeeping purposes, but are also useful for catching cups and straws."

"And finally," she finished, "Mark 1 now has Interactive Smart Toes. They allow full rotation of each digit, to finetune his kicking action on contact with the ball. In other words: when he shoots, he can't miss."

Harvey heard Darren whisper, "Now he's got everything — and he's lucky, too!"

"Mark 1 has a single purpose — to train

you all into becoming the ultimate team," said Professor Gertie. "I wanted him to be a surprise."

"But aren't you cross about The Team wearing their barebones?" Harvey asked Professor Gertie delicately.

"That won't be a problem for much longer," she said mysteriously.

Harvey was puzzled, but the rest of The Team didn't look troubled. So Harvey decided to push all thoughts of barebones and jinxes from his mind. The Team were back together. And they were going to play.

A referee Harvey hadn't seen before walked on to the field. Her whistle was already at her lips.

"Let's go, *Superstars*," Harvey said.

And that was when it all started to go wrong again.

As Harvey and Rita prepared to kick off, the referee jogged around The Team, removing their barebones and putting them in her pocket. "Jewellery is not safe to be worn whilst playing," she said.

The Team looked at each other in dismay.

Then Harvey saw something he would never have thought possible. Mark 1 pulled on a stripy shirt, like some of the Odds and Ends players wore, and joined the other team.

"That makes a full set of players," said the Odds and Ends captain, amazed. "We never get that many — it must be our lucky day!"

"Mark 1's supposed to be helping *us*!" Rita breathed weakly.

Darren chased after the referee. "Barebones aren't jewellery!" he told her. "They're for good luck against the jinx! And Mark 1's not allowed to play! He's a robot!"

The referee looked from Darren to Mark 1 before saying cheerfully, "I don't believe in jinxes. And anyone or anything can play for the Odds and Ends."

Darren bellowed with frustration.

And just when he thought things couldn't get any worse, Harvey felt his lucky undershorts becoming dangerously hot.

Chapter 6

When the referee blew her whistle to start the game, Harvey jumped. He'd been concentrating on what was happening in his shorts.

He tapped the ball to Rita, but she backed away as if she was scared to touch it. Then . . .

Whoooom!

Mark 1 zoomed past, collected the ball, and streaked like a missile towards The Team's goal.

"Stop him!" Harvey appealed to The Team. But everyone looked too scared to move.

"*Noooo!*" Darren cried. Instead of spreading himself in the goal, he wrapped his head in his arms and made himself as small as he could.

Mark 1 sent the ball curling like a frisbee into the top corner, before doing celebratory cartwheels back towards his cheering team. "Eeeezie goalll!" he sang.

"One–nil to the Odds and Ends!" said the referee. "The Team kick off."

The Team were still standing in their starting positions.

Harvey hadn't even strayed from the centre spot. He looked pleadingly at Rita. "We've just got to try," he said.

"I can't do anything!" Rita replied. "The referee took my barebone!"

The Odds and Ends began to complain about time wasting.

Darren ran up to Harvey. "Are you still wearing the underpants?" he said desperately. "They're our only hope."

Harvey lowered his shorts a little — and heard a shout of outrage from the sidelines.

"Harvey Boots!" screeched Professor Gertie. "Take off my Match Day Bloomers!"

"You mean those pants don't belong to Mark 1?" said Darren, turning pale.

"Help me get them off!" said Harvey, who wanted nothing more than to give the undershorts back to their owner.

The Team made a screen for Harvey, who removed the Match Day Bloomers and handed them back to Professor Gertie. She held up the shorts and examined them.

"They will need to be recharged," she concluded.

"Recharged?" said Harvey. "I didn't do anything, honest!"

"You have used up the noise-activated Heat-Up Stitches. Something must have set them off."

Harvey was keen to change the subject. "We've got to try and block Mark 1," he said to his team mates. "We can't even think about attack, only defence."

The referee blew her whistle again, tapping her watch.

"We have to —" Harvey began, but Steffi cut him off.

"We have to *do nothing*," she said. "It's too dangerous to play now that we have no lucky charms. We're jinxed, remember?"

"There has to be something we can do . . ." said Rita.

"There isn't," said Darren. "We can't break the jinx."

"Let's go home, then," said Matt.

The Team turned to go. Then they stopped. They looked at each other, but nobody took another step.

Harvey found himself smiling. "We can't give up," he said. "We never gave up during our first season, when we lost every game for months. And we won't give up now. We're The Team. We keep going. *No matter what.*"

The Team still didn't move. A third shrill whistle told them that the referee was running out of patience.

Harvey eyed each of his team mates. "Who's up for it?" he said.

Nobody spoke.

Then, as one, The Team returned to their positions on the pitch. Their shoulders were

slumped and they looked beaten. But, Harvey thought, we've never been quitters.

Harvey kicked off to Rita — and, just as before, Mark 1 pounced on the ball.

This time the robot passed to an Odds and Ends striker. The Team retreated to defend their goal. Darren's eyes were wide with fear, but he stood tall, hollering instructions to his defenders as the Odds and Ends slowly built an attack.

Suddenly, a shot from Mark 1 rocketed at Darren. He reacted instinctively and parried it away, only to see it volleyed back by the robot. The second shot was beyond his reach.

Harvey drew in a breath — conceding a goal now would rock The Team's confidence even further. But to his relief, Steffi blocked the ball on the line, and Matt booted it clear.

For the rest of the first half, Mark 1 fired a barrage of lightning-fast shots, and The Team blocked them bravely with their feet, heads and bodies.

And that, thought Harvey, was a lot better than nothing. "It's not pretty," he said at half-time, "but at least we're only losing by one goal."

They sat down by Professor Gertie, who handed out drink bottles.

"The worst part of all this is that we can't

fight back against Mark 1," said Darren moodily.

"That traitor!" said Steffi.

"He's not a traitor," said Harvey immediately.

"What's he up to then?" asked Matt.

Harvey couldn't answer.

"Why is Mark 1 playing against us, Professor?" said Rita. "He's supposed to be our trainer."

The Team watched the robot showing off his Rapid Reflex arms to the Odds and Ends by juggling slices of orange.

"I suppose it might be his new A.I.," said Professor Gertie awkwardly.

"What's that?" said Harvey.

"Arty Intelligence," explained Professor Gertie. "It allows him to be creative and think for himself. I installed his Trillion-Gig A.I. Unit the day before The Team thrashed the Diamonds."

"That was when Mark 1 told me about the Superstars record," said Darren dejectedly. "Now I wish he hadn't bothered."

"I thought you found out about the record yourself," said Harvey.

"I did, in a way," said Darren. "Mark 1 was in the library, too. He showed me the old newspaper with the picture of the Odds and Ends being Superstars. The writing under the picture was all about the jinx."

"Hang on!" Rita said. She got to her feet and began pacing up and down. "You don't think Mark 1 has been against us ever since he got his Arty Intelligence, do you?"

"He's not against us," said Harvey, but The Team ignored him.

"What if," Rita mused, "Mark 1 started by making us believe we were jinxed?"

"Mark 1 can't have made all those accidents happen in training," argued Harvey. "He wasn't even there."

Rita thought for a moment, then sighed. "Maybe they *were* just accidents after all," she said. "I might have twisted my ankle because I didn't warm up properly."

Steffi spoke from the edge of the group. "That wasn't the first time Matt has got in my way," she admitted. "He does it all the time."

"Same to you," said Matt.

"There's been a nasty crack in the crossbar for weeks," Darren mused. "It was going to break one of these days. And your ball was pretty old, Harvey — it had worn thin."

"We only believed we were jinxed because Darren had read about it in the newspaper that Mark 1 showed him," said Rita.

"What about the barebones?" said Matt. "Why did Mark 1 give us those?"

"Mark 1 wanted us to think that wearing them was the only way to ward off the jinx," said Rita.

Darren frowned. "And he made his barebones look even luckier by taking us on that hike!" he said furiously.

Professor Gertie spoke grimly. "Mark 1 must have known the referee would take the barebones away during the match. Even I knew that."

"Mark 1 guessed that without our barebones, we'd be too scared to play properly against his new team," said Rita. "The Odds and Ends couldn't lose."

There was a silence as The Team let Rita's words sink in.

"You've got to be joking!" said Harvey. "Mark 1's always been on our side!"

"He was — before Professor Gertie gave him A.I.," said Rita. "You have to face it, Harvey. Mark 1 has changed."

"He's the enemy now," said Darren, gritting his teeth.

Harvey still didn't believe it. "Only a genius could work out a plan like that!"

"Mark 1 *is* a genius," said Professor Gertie bleakly. "And if he's determined to beat The Team, nothing can stop him."

Chapter 7

"Tell me one thing, Professor," said Steffi, sounding dangerously calm. "If barebones aren't lucky charms, then what are they?"

"Barebones are used-up parts of Mark 1's internal circuitry," said Professor Gertie. "They fall out of him from time to time."

Rita gulped. "You mean . . . we were wearing bits of Mark 1's *waste*?" She rubbed around her neck as if to clean it.

"That's disgusting!" said Darren. "I wore mine in bed!"

"They're not lucky charms, then?" said Steffi.

"No," said Professor Gertie.

"Right," said Steffi. And to Harvey's surprise, she began to shove him onto the pitch. "Let's go," she said quietly. "Move it."

Harvey could feel her hands trembling, and saw spots of red on her cheeks. An image of a hot volcano, about to blow at any moment, came into his mind. He watched her grab Matt and Darren by their collars, and yank them to their feet.

"Gerroff!" Darren said. "We're not playing!"

And then Steffi erupted. Her arms flew up in the air. She tipped her head back. And she shrieked, "If you think I'm letting that no-good rust-bucket get away with his fun and games, then you can think again!" She drew in a long, ragged breath, before continuing, "We're going to teach that robot something he doesn't know and has not yet learned — not to mess with The Team!"

Steffi deposited Matt and Darren on the field, and made the rest of The Team follow.

Then she stood in the centre of defence, looking as solid as a rock.

Matt chortled. "She spent all week showing off her barebone!" he explained. "When her trendy friends find out what a barebone really is, she'll never live it down!"

Harvey was sure he could see steam rising from Steffi's ears as she glared at Mark 1.

At the referee's signal, the robot kicked off. Then he darted forward to receive the ball.

When he did, Steffi was ready for him. She leapt to bodycheck Mark 1 in midair.

CRUNCH!

The robot was knocked sideways. A cheer went up from The Team as Steffi claimed the ball. But Mark 1 was still on his feet.

Swivel! Turn! went his Spinner.

Steffi barely had a moment to act before the robot closed in on her.

"To me!" Harvey said, finding space. Steffi sidefooted the ball to him just in time. Harvey had only a split second to pass to Matt before the robot whirred past him at top speed. "Keep the ball to ourselves!" Harvey yelled.

Matt did as he was told, backheeling the ball to Rita, who knocked it on to Harvey. Matt began cheering every pass — but Harvey was painfully aware that they weren't facing Masher this time. Mark 1 was the perfect Football Machine, and he was pushing his formidable skills to the limit.

But try as he might, Mark 1 couldn't steal the ball from The Team.

The minutes ticked past.

Suddenly, Harvey realised that all the Odds

and Ends were in The Team's half of the pitch. Their keeper had left his goal undefended as he watched their new star player in action.

"Kick it *forwards*, okay?" Harvey told Rita.

Rita nodded doubtfully, but when Darren flung the ball towards her, she kicked it far into their opponents' half.

Harvey hurled himself after the ball. He could hear the *whizz-wazz* of Mark 1's leg-motors getting louder as the robot caught him up.

Whizz-wazz, WHIZZ-WAZZ!

Harvey reached the ball first and, without pausing, fired goalwards. He watched his shot

curl almost as much as Mark 1's had. The ball slammed inside the top corner of the goal — and stayed there. It was stuck firmly in the angle between the crossbar and the post.

Harvey gasped.

"I have *never* seen that before," the referee said. "The ball hasn't crossed the line. Bad luck!"

Harvey felt his energy drain away as the Odds and Ends goalkeeper reached up to pull the ball down and throw it to Mark 1.

The robot galloped down the left wing, then swerved in towards Darren's goal.

Harvey trudged back to the halfway line, watching helplessly.

The Team couldn't win. There was nothing they could do to change that fact.

Their luck had run out.

He saw Professor Gertie cover her eyes.

And then —

SLAM! SKID! THUD! CLANG!

The Team intercepted from all sides, tackling, blocking, and cutting off the robot as they surged together. Harvey had never seen defence like it. Mark 1 was sent tumbling to the ground from a superb sliding tackle, and Rita sped away with the ball. She sent it skimming upfield to Harvey, who ran forwards, skipped past the goalkeeper, and blasted the ball safely into the middle of the Odds and Ends' net.

"GOAL!" shouted Harvey.

The Team were brilliant, he realised, as his friends hurtled towards him in celebration.

They stuck together, just like they had on the hike.

They worked hard together, just as they had against Masher.

And they were brave, battling against a football-genius robot, even though luck was against them.

No matter how difficult things were, they kept on . . .

Suddenly, Harvey finally understood what Mark 1 had been up to from the start.

The referee ended the game, calling, "It's a draw. One goal each!"

Harvey walked away from The Team's celebrations to where Mark 1 was sitting on the ground. The robot was looking dazed but happy.

"Thanks," Harvey said to Mark 1. "You were perfect."

The rest of The Team and Professor Gertie hurried over to Harvey.

"What are you on about?" said Darren. "Mark 1 is against us — we had to raise our game to the top to stop him!"

"I know," said Harvey. *"And it's made us the best we've ever been.* He's been doing what he was made to do — training us!"

Mark 1's eyes flashed.

"You mean Rita was right?" said Steffi. "Mark 1 planned everything?"

"Yes," said Harvey. "Mark 1 pretended to be against us so that we'd learn how to beat the most formidable opponent we're ever likely to meet: him! It was Mark 1's way of making us a stronger team!"

The Team gawped at the robot — and then, as one, they began to applaud.

Professor Gertie wiped a tear from her eye. "What a clever-cogs he is!" she said fondly.

The Odds and Ends captain came to shake Mark 1's hand. "We learned a lot today," he told Harvey. "We saw how you play as a team. The Odds and Ends used to play like that, a long time ago. But after we won a record, all our best players were poached by other teams. That just left a bunch of strangers."

"So you weren't jinxed, then?" said Darren.

"No," said the captain. "The jinx was just a story in the newspaper."

Darren sighed. "Looks like I got it wrong," he said miserably.

"We all did," said Steffi.

"From now on," announced Matt. "I'm making my own luck."

"We should all be able to do that," said Rita. "We are *Superstars*, after all."

"And we're The Team," said Harvey, grinning as his team mates lifted Mark 1 and Professor Gertie onto their shoulders. "Always — and forever!"